Ramadan in Space

By
Moni Z.

Illustrated by
Ahmed & Zaki A.

For my Sons, and all the children who are complete Space enthusiasts, and have a desire to share and learn about lives on Earth and beyond. Enjoy!

Are You Ready for a Journey to the Stars...

Up and Away

My name is Ahmed
And I'm on a mission
That's extraordinary
I'm excited to travel
To the planet, that is MARS
In my blue and red spaceship
On a journey, through the stars

3, 2, 1... Blast off
My spaceship takes off
As I look out the window
And see the Earth fly past
Like a giant blue sphere
Its pitch black, out there
Except for little shiny dots
Which are stars that glare

I'm extra charged, to travel in space
Cuz' I'm meeting a family, up at their place
Which happens to be, on the planet MARS
It's indeed a planet, much different than ours

They are very nice people
But they haven't met me before
So it's my duty to share
What they don't know
The kind of people we are
It's on me, to let it show

So here we are, on MARS I land
I see a family, just like we are
Mom, dad and three jumpy kids, not
too far
'You look just like us', I exclaim in
delight
My mind is filled up with ideas bright
Of play dates and picnics, together on
MARS
Of hide and seek, and endless
playtime with cars

They take me to places, grooviest of
all
Imagine, Jell-O filled ponds as
skating rinks
And trampolines set up in the craters
of MARS
In the night time, we watch an
Aurora* show
Imagine the sky, with red and green
glow

I tell them, I'd love to spend some
more time
But right now, I need to reach back
home
As *Ramadan starts in just a few days
more
'Ramadan? What's that? Sounds
totally fun!'
Little Martian kid there, cheerfully
begun
'Yes it is!' I say, 'How'd you guess?'
I dearly confess...
'Well here's what, I'd like you to know
I am a Muslim, from the planet Earth
There are around 1.7 billion of us
Who believe in one GOD
He has created us all
The Earth that we know
And MARS as well
And that we have a purpose
To be honest, to be good
And be good to others

Ramadan is a month when Muslims
fast
And stop eating or drinking from
morning to dusk
For the will of One God, whose favors
are vast

This is the month of forgiveness for
all
It teaches us patience, and Self
Control

Ramadan, is togetherness at its best
Sitting down for Sehr*, and Iftaar* at
Sunset
Dates, nuts, milk and fruit salad
Make our wait, all the more valid

Some of us are lucky to have that all
But we have to care for the ones, who
do not
By inviting them over Iftaar, at our
place
Or cook for them nice meals, at other
days

Ramadan is the time of family nights
Prayers at the mosque, called
Taraweeh*
To recharge and gain spirituality

The fun walks to the mosque, with
dad & mom
And the brothers who are annoying,
and at the same time fun

And after Ramadan it's EID, the
festival
It's best of the best, I tell you for sure
There are morning prayers, fun rides,
and carnival

So all in all, it's a time not to miss
If you happen to be Earth bound,
then I invite you to this
To come spend a Ramadan, on our
planet blue
Who knows it falls during your
summer vacation too

And with that, I spent the fun-est of
times
My adventures are endless, but I need
to sleep
I'll save those stories, for the next
time we meet!

Ramadan Kareem

Glossary and References

*Ramadan: Ramadan is one of the holiest months of the Islamic year, when Muslims fast, pray, and help those around them, who are in need. Ramadan is the ninth month of the Islamic calendar, and is observed by Muslims worldwide as a month of fasting to commemorate the first revelation of the Quran to Prophet Muhammad (Peace be upon him) according to Islamic belief. This annual observance is regarded as one of the Five Pillars of Islam. The month lasts 29–30 days based on the visual sightings of the crescent moon, according to numerous biographical accounts compiled in the hadiths.

*Aurora: An aurora, sometimes referred to as a polar light, is a natural light display in the sky, predominantly seen in the high latitude (Arctic and Antarctic) regions.

Aurora Reference in Poem:
New Discovery - NASA Spacecraft Detects Aurora and Mysterious Dust Cloud around Mars

*Sehr: Suhūr (suhūr, lit. "of the dawn", "pre-dawn meal"; also spelled suhoor, sahur, or sehri) is an Islamic term referring to the meal consumed early in the morning by Muslims before fasting, sawm, before dawn during or outside the Islamic month of Ramadan. The meal is eaten before fajr prayer.

*Iftaar: Iftar (iftār 'breakfast') is the evening meal when Muslims end their daily Ramadan fast at sunset.

*Taraweeh: Taraweeh refers to extra prayers performed by Muslims at night in the Islamic month of Ramadan.

(Above info courtesy wikipedia.org)

Thanks for spending time with us. Until we meet again!

Space Notes

_____

_____

_____

_____

_____

_____

_____

_____

_____

_____

_____

Made in the USA
Middletown, DE
25 March 2017